# Milly
### the River
## Fairy

For the lovely
Milly Johnson — surprise!

Special thanks to Sue Mongredin

ISBN 978-0-545-60529-8

Previously published as Green Fairies #6: *Milly the River Fairy* by Orchard U.K. in 2009.

All rights reserved. Published by Scholastic Inc., 557 Broadway, New York, NY 10012, by arrangement with Rainbow Magic Limited.

12 11 10 9 8 7 6 5 4 3 2 1          14 15 16 17 18 19/0

Printed in the U.S.A.          40

This edition first printing, July 2014

# Milly
## the River
## Fairy

by Daisy Meadows

SCHOLASTIC INC.

The Earth Fairies must be dreaming
If they think they can escape my scheming.
My goblins are by far the greenest,
And I am definitely the meanest.

Seven fairies out to save the earth?
This very idea fills me with mirth!
I'm sure the world has had enough
Of fairy magic and all that stuff.

So I'm going to steal the fairies' wands
And send them into human lands.
The fairies will think all is lost,
Defeated again—by me, Jack Frost!

# Contents

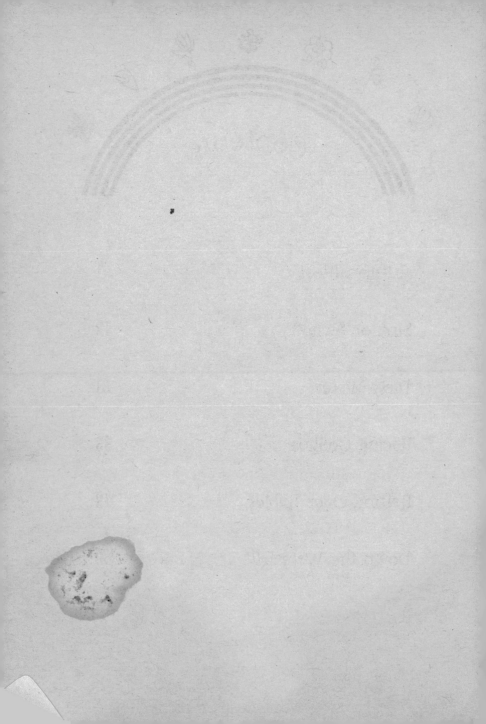

# A Fairy Afloat

"It's definitely colder than yesterday," Rachel Walker said as she and her best friend, Kirsty Tate, strolled through Rainspell Park. "I can't believe we were so warm on the beach at the start of the week—and today we're all wrapped up in our cozy sweaters!"

Kirsty grinned at Rachel. "And I can't believe we were swimming in the ocean with Coral the Reef Fairy a few days ago," she said in a low voice. "Imagine how freezing cold the water must be right now!"

Rachel shivered at the thought. "She'd have to use a *lot* of fairy magic to keep us warm today, wouldn't she?"

The two girls smiled at each other as they walked through the

park. It was the fall break, and they were both here on Rainspell Island for a week with their parents. Rainspell Island was the place where Kirsty and Rachel had first met. They'd shared a very special summer together . . . and now this vacation was turning out to be every bit as magical!

"Oh, I love being friends with the fairies," Kirsty said happily, thinking about all the exciting adventures they'd had so far.

"We really are the luckiest girls in the world, Rachel."

"Definitely," Rachel agreed. Golden-brown leaves tumbled from the trees every time the wind blew, and Rachel noticed just then that some of the trees were already bare. "Well, it's certainly windy enough today to sail our boats," she said as a yellow leaf floated down and landed at her feet. She glanced at the paper boat she was holding. Both girls had made one back at their cottage that morning. "They're going to speed along with this breeze behind them."

"Here's the lake," Kirsty said as they rounded a corner and saw the stretch of blue water ahead of them. She held up her own paper boat and raised an eyebrow at Rachel. "Mine is going to be the fastest, you know."

Rachel laughed. "No way!" she insisted.

The two girls had decorated their boats with

felt tip pens and they were bright and colorful. Kirsty's was red and gold, and she'd written *Autumn Spirit* along one side of it. Rachel had colored hers pink and lilac, and had called it *Magical Mist.* As they reached the water's edge, both girls set their boats down carefully on the surface, and watched them float away. A gust of wind blew the boats straight ahead, and Kirsty and Rachel cheered as the tiny vessels sailed quickly toward the middle of the lake.

"Go, go, *Autumn Spirit*!" Kirsty cried.
"Let's run around to the other side of
the lake so we can catch them as they
come in," Rachel suggested.

The girls sprinted along the path that circled the lake, making sure they checked on their boats every now and then. When the path led them back to the lake, the girls scanned the water to see where their boats had gone.

Then Kirsty let out a cry of dismay. "Oh, no! Look, Rachel! There's a tire sticking out of the water—and our boats are heading straight for it. They'll get stuck for sure!"

Rachel opened her mouth to reply, but then noticed something else. "Kirsty, have you seen who's standing on your boat?" she cried. "It's Milly the River Fairy!"

Kirsty looked at her boat, thrilled at the thought of another fairy adventure. Sure enough, there was Milly, one of seven fairies she and Rachel had met at the start of the week. Milly had long honey-colored hair, with a braid around the front. She wore a pretty blue-green top and a matching skirt, both made of flowing, shimmering fabric.

Queen Titania and King Oberon had
given seven fairies-in-training the title of
"Earth Fairies" for a trial period. The
fairies had the special mission of helping
humans look after the environment. Milly
was one of the chosen Earth Fairies, as
were six others named Nicole, Isabella,
Edie, Coral, Lily, and Carrie.
Unfortunately, just as the new Earth
Fairies were about to be given their magic
wands, wicked Jack Frost and his goblins
had appeared and snatched them away.

"I'm sure my goblins will give the
words *being green* a whole new meaning,"
Jack Frost had said with a sneer. And
then he and his goblins vanished into the
human world, where they'd been causing
all kinds of trouble with the magic
wands ever since.

Fortunately, Kirsty and Rachel had been able to help five of the fairies get back their stolen wands, but two of the wands were still missing — the ones that belonged to Milly the River Fairy and Carrie the Snow Cap Fairy.

Milly was smiling and waving at them now from where she stood on Kirsty's boat. But Kirsty didn't smile back. "Oh, no," she said, seized by a jolt of fear. "I don't think Milly sees that tire — and the boat's going to crash into it any second. If it bumps too hard, the boat will sink!"

# Sink or Swim?

Kirsty began waving her arms frantically above her head, trying to warn the little fairy. "Watch out!" she yelled. "Milly, get off the boat!"

But the wind was so strong it carried Kirsty's words away, and Milly didn't seem to hear. She clearly thought Kirsty was just being friendly, so she smiled and waved back at her.

"If Milly gets knocked into the water and her wings get wet, she won't be able to fly," Rachel realized. How horrible! "Milly! You're going to crash!" she yelled, waving like Kirsty.

It was no good. Milly went on waving and smiling back at them . . . until moments later, when Kirsty's boat hit the tire with a bump. Then Rachel's boat blew straight into Kirsty's—and they both wobbled dangerously on the waves.

"They're sinking!" Kirsty cried in horror as she saw water splashing over the edge of her boat. It leaned to one side . . . but luckily, just as it was about to flip over, the girls saw Milly dart up into the air, her wings fluttering furiously as she zoomed away from the boats.

Down went the boats. Their colored sides became soggy within moments. Milly flew over to the girls, her face blank and pale.

"Are you OK?" Rachel asked, seeing the little fairy shivering all over. "We were trying to warn you about that tire but . . ."

Milly managed a smile. "Don't feel bad, it's not your fault," she said in a silvery voice. "That tire should never have been in the lake in the first place. Since King Oberon and Queen Titania made me the fairy in charge of looking after rivers and waterways, I've been finding out just how bad water pollution is around the world. I really need to find my wand so that I can make the rivers and lakes cleaner."

Kirsty bit her lip. "And now our paper boats have added to the litter in the lake," she said, looking sad. "I'm really sorry, Milly. We didn't think."

Milly fluttered over to perch on Kirsty's shoulder. "What's done is done," she said kindly. "And it wasn't your fault the boats crashed and sank. It's all the more reason why I should get my wand back!"

"Well, we'll certainly help you," Rachel said at once. She remembered that King Oberon and Queen Titania had promised that if the Earth Fairies were successful during their trial period, they would be given the roles permanently. The more she and Kirsty learned about environmental issues, the more it sounded as if the world really needed some dedicated Earth Fairies to help clean it up.

"Thanks," Milly said, smiling at Rachel. "I have an idea about where my wand is. With the small amount of magic I have, I can take us all there now, if you'd like."

"Of course," Kirsty said at once. "There's nobody around to see us. Let's go!"

Milly sprinkled the girls with some glittering turquoise fairy dust, which made them shrink to her size. Next, delicate fairy wings appeared on their backs.

Milly threw another handful of fairy dust over them all, and Kirsty and Rachel found themselves surrounded by a sparkling golden whirlwind that whisked them higher in the air.

Rachel managed to grab Kirsty's hand as they rose up in the golden mist. She clung to her friend, breathless with excitement. They were off on another fairy adventure!

# Dirty Water

After a short time, Kirsty and Rachel
felt their feet touch the ground once
more, and the sparkly whirlwind cleared.
They looked around and found that
they were next to a wide river that
had grassy banks on either side. The
water in the river was clear and blue. It
sparkled in the sunlight as it flowed
along. Huge trees lined the riverbanks.
Their red and gold leaves cast bright
reflections in the river.

"It's beautiful here." Rachel sighed.
"Oh, look! Is that a deer?"

They all turned to see where Rachel
was pointing. Kirsty held her breath as
the deer emerged from between the trees.
The creature looked young and anxious,
her wide eyes checking this
way and that for danger as
she trotted toward the
river. The sun glinted
off her reddish-brown
coat as she bent her
head gracefully to
drink the water.

Elsewhere, a group
of squirrels was playing
in a large beech tree.
They scampered up and
down the trunk, and swung

from the branches like fluffy miniature
acrobats. Little pink-and-white flowers
grew in clumps around the trees, and
birds called to one another. Kirsty and
Rachel couldn't stop smiling at the scene
before them. It really seemed like a
perfect place!

Milly had tensed slightly. She seemed to be listening for something. Then she smiled, too. "My wand *is* near here, I can sense it," she said. "Come on, let's fly down the river and see if we can find it." Rachel, Kirsty, and Milly fluttered up in the air and followed the river. After a few minutes of flying they rounded a bend in the river, and the scene changed abruptly. Ahead stood a big factory with smoke pouring from its chimneys. The sound of loud, rumbling machinery filled the air. Even worse, there was a dirty yellow scum on the surface of the water. *"Ugh!"* cried Rachel, wrinkling her nose. "Why does the river look like that?"

Milly sighed. "The factory pumps its waste straight into here," she said sadly. "That's a really bad thing. The waste makes the water harmful to drink, and the fish living in the river get sick or die. The waste can also kill some of the plants that live in the river."

Kirsty felt upset hearing this. "That's awful," she said, noticing the way the yellow scum on the water clung to the edge of the grassy riverbank as it flowed past. And it smelled horrible, too—a nasty, chemical kind of smell.

"Yes," Rachel agreed, then she put her hands on her hips. "Well, it makes it even more important for us to find Milly's wand and get it back for her, so that she can do something to clean up this river—and all the others like it."

"Yes," said Milly. "And—" Then she stopped. "Oh, no," she cried, pointing ahead. "We've got to stop that deer. Hurry!"

She flew off at top speed, and Kirsty and Rachel realized why: The deer was heading toward this part of the river. If the deer drank from the dirty water, she could get sick. Milly used her magic to cast a spell so that she would be able to talk to the deer. Flapping their wings as hard as they could, Kirsty and Rachel flew after the little fairy.

"Don't drink that!" Milly called out, swooping toward the animal, who was just bending her head down to the water.

"Please! It's polluted—really dirty and full of bad chemicals. It might make you sick if you swallow it."

The deer raised her head and blinked her large brown eyes at the sight of Milly, and Rachel and Kirsty, who were just behind their fairy friend. Then she gazed down at the water with a sad look on her face. "Thank you for the warning," she said. "My name's Dotty."

"I'm Milly, and this is Kirsty and Rachel," the fairy said. "There's some fresh, clean water farther upstream, once you get past this smelly factory. It'll be much nicer to drink than this."

Dotty smiled at her and bobbed her head. "Thank you," she said again. "Usually I drink farther down the river, but there are some very strange creatures there today, making a lot of noise. I was a little scared of them, so thought I'd come here instead."

Rachel's ears perked up at the deer's words. "What kind of strange creatures?" she asked.

Dotty gave a shudder. "Horrible, shouty creatures," she said. "They're like little green men, and they're sailing on the river, frightening all the animals with their screaming and hollering."

"Little green men?" Kirsty echoed, her eyes lighting up. "I think we know who they are."

"Goblins!" cried Rachel and Milly.

# Racing Goblins

"Dotty, you're the best," Milly said, patting the deer's black nose.

"I am?" Dotty asked, looking puzzled.

"You are." Kirsty smiled. "Thank you. We have to fly now. Good-bye!"

Kirsty, Rachel, and Milly set off, following the river again as it wound its way through the woodland. They left the factory behind, and the water began to become clear again. It also became much faster, Rachel noticed. In fact, after a while, the current of the river was so strong that the water was positively rushing along below them, splashing and bubbling as it tumbled over the rocky riverbed.

A short time later, they heard high-pitched shrieks and excited cheers. "That's definitely the goblins," said Milly. "But what are they doing?"

It wasn't long before the three fairies found out. When they rounded the next bend in the river they saw four goblins racing along on homemade rafts, two on each one.

"Look what that goblin is holding,"
Milly exclaimed, pointing down at them.
"My wand!"

Kirsty and Rachel saw that a goblin
with a big nose had a sparkly magic
wand in his hand. He was using it to
show the other goblins which way they
should sail.

"Straight ahead!" they heard him
shout. "*Wheeee!* This is fun."

"Let's hide in this tree and make a plan," Milly suggested in a low voice. "The goblins don't know that we've found them—we should keep it that way for as long as we can."

"Good thinking," Rachel said as they perched on a leafy branch. "If they don't know we're here, we can surprise them."

Kirsty nodded. "They're focusing so hard on racing that they're only looking ahead, and not up in the air." She leaned over slightly to watch the noisy goblins. "Maybe if we dive straight down from above, we'll be able to catch them off guard and grab the wand before they even know we're there."

"Yay!" Rachel cheered. "They won't know what hit them."

Milly seemed to like the idea, too. "As soon as I touch the wand, it'll shrink to its Fairyland size, so I'll easily be able to carry it away," she said. "Let's do it!"

The three fairies set off, swooping high

above the goblins on their rafts. The
goblins had obviously built the rafts
themselves out of pieces of garbage,
Kirsty realized. One seemed to be made
of planks tied to some big plastic
barrels, while the other
was made of wooden
poles that had
been wound
together with
twine. The goblins
were using flat
pieces of wood
as paddles.

The big-
nosed goblin was holding the wand in
front of him. "Keep going," he said
bossily. "There's a bend coming up,
make sure you steer into it, remember."

The goblin sitting next to him rolled his eyes. "All right, all right, Captain Hook," he muttered under his breath.

The goblin with the wand scowled. "I told you not to call me that!" he snapped. Kirsty and Rachel had to press their hands to their mouths to stop themselves from giggling.

"I think this might be a good time to grabthe wand," Milly suggested with a grin. "Here I go. . . ." Down she plunged, arms pointed straight in front of her as she flew. Kirsty and Rachel watched in excitement. *For once, this is actually going to be easy,* Rachel thought with a smile.

But just as she was about to say as much to Kirsty, both rafts knocked into a boulder in the middle of the river with a bump. The goblin holding the wand staggered, trying to regain his balance. The wand went flying out of his hand!

Milly made a dive for it, but she was too late . . . and the wand landed in the water with a splash. She gasped.

A look of horror spread over Milly's face. "The wand's floating away," she cried to Kirsty and Rachel. "Come on—we've got to find it before it's lost forever. Follow that wand!"

# Rafting Over Rapids

The goblins looked up in annoyance as they heard Milly's shout. "Fairies? Yuck!" wailed a tall goblin. "They're after our wand, I bet. Well, we can't let them get it!"

"No way!" agreed a short, squat goblin with a mean face. "Jack Frost will be really angry if we lose it. Come on, paddle harder. We've got to get that wand back!"

The goblins threw themselves whole-heartedly into their paddling, and their rafts sped along after the wand.

Overhead, the three fairies were chasing after it, too. Fortunately, the wand was easy to follow, because it left behind a trail of golden sparkles, but the fast current meant it rushed along with the water at top speed.

"I think we should fly closer to the river," Rachel called to Milly and Kirsty. "That way we can grab the wand as soon as we get near it."

"Good thinking," Kirsty replied, and they swooped down, so that they just skimmed the water as they zoomed along.

Flying so fast was really exciting, but the three friends hadn't planned on there being so much trash floating in the river. It was hard work having to dodge around empty bottles and plastic bags.

"There's so much litter!" Rachel cried, swerving quickly in order to avoid a broken umbrella caught against a rock. Its spokes were sharp and pointed, and her heart pounded as she almost collided with it.

"I know, it's disgusting," Kirsty said, flying over yet another wrinkled plastic bag.

"We've got to get to that wand before

the goblins do. This river needs a serious
cleanup."

"Oh, no!" Milly suddenly said
nervously. "Have you seen what's ahead?
Rapids!"

Kirsty and Rachel gulped as they saw
what she meant.
The river was
now flowing
steeply
downhill,
causing the
water to turn
white and
foamy as it
churned
over the
rocks.

The goblins looked anxious, too. Their

rafts were wildly bobbing up and down
with the strong current, and the tall
goblin looked
very seasick. His
eyes were closed
as he clung
to the raft.

Just then, the
magic wand
was flipped on its
end by the bubbling water, so that it was
carried along with its tip in the air.

"Quick!" cried Kirsty, soaring toward
it. She grabbed ahold of it, as did Rachel,
and together, they pulled it out of the
water.

"Yes!" Kirsty cried. "We got it, Milly!"

Milly let out a cheer. Then, just as she
was flying over to grab it, the goblins on

the barrel-and-plank raft raced by. The big-nosed goblin snatched the wand right out of Rachel's and Kirsty's fingers!

"Hey!" Rachel yelled. "Give that back!"

"No way," he chided, twirling it between his fingers. "I won't let it go again . . . whoa!"

His raft was bumping and bouncing even harder on the wild current, and the goblin fell sideways. With a shout of fear, he reached for a nearby rope to hold on to. When he did so, the wand slipped from his fingers and splashed down into the water again.

"No!" the short goblin

bellowed, shaking his fist. "You can't be
trusted with anything!"

"It's not my fault," the big-nosed goblin
yelled back. "You suggested making
these rafts in the first place. This is all
*your* fault." He stopped and looked ahead
in shock.

The short goblin was just about to
shout a reply when he also glanced
ahead—and yelled in terror.
"Waterfall!" he screamed. "Help!"

# Down the Waterfall!

The two rafts plunged over the waterfall, and the goblins fell off immediately, wailing and shrieking as they tumbled through the air. The wand was falling, too. As the fairy friends flew through the mist of the roaring waterfall, Rachel managed to veer over and grab the wand out of midair. It was heavy for a little fairy, though, and the weight of the wand immediately pulled her down.

"Milly!" she called above the noise of the water as it crashed below them. "Here!"

Milly zoomed over at once, her hand outstretched, and grabbed hold of the wand. As soon as Milly touched it, the wand shrank down to fairy-size. With a few good flaps, Rachel was able to get a safe distance above the rushing waterfall again. *Whew!* She sighed in relief.

Meanwhile, Milly was waving the wand in the goblins' direction, muttering some magic words. A stream of golden sparkles shot from the wand and swirled around the goblins . . . just in time to make them land safely on their rafts at the bottom of the waterfall.

"Now to guide them safely to the shore," Milly said with another flourish of her wand. Once again, a flurry of golden sparkles streamed from it, and the two rafts were magically steered to the river bank. The goblins climbed onto land  with shaky legs. All four of them looked sopping wet and utterly miserable.

"I think you'd better go back to Jack Frost's castle now and dry off," Milly called sweetly, hovering above them with Rachel and Kirsty on either side of her.

The goblins all glared, but said

nothing. They trudged away, heads
down, bickering among themselves.
They knew when they were beaten.

Milly flung her arms around
Rachel and
Kirsty.
"Thank
you, girls!"
she cried.
"I don't
think I've
ever flown
quite so fast
in my life."

Kirsty grinned.
"That was really exciting," she said.
"Glad we could help."

Milly eyed the river and then her
wand. "Now . . . I have work to do,

don't I?" she said. "Come on!"

The three of them flew up to the top of the waterfall, and back to where the water was still polluted from the factory waste. Milly waved her wand over the river. As she did so, the dirty scum vanished from the surface and

the plastic bags and other items of litter disappeared. Kirsty and Rachel cheered, but Milly still looked troubled. "Well, it's clean for the time being, but it's up to you humans now. You have to stop factories from dumping waste in the river, and you need to put trash in garbage cans and recycling bins. It doesn't belong here."

"You're right," Rachel said. "We have to work together."

"There's Dotty again," Kirsty said, suddenly noticing the pretty deer they'd met earlier. "Let's tell her the good news."

They flew over to greet Dotty, who promptly drank from the clean water. "Delicious," she said. "Thank you!"

"My pleasure," Milly replied. "And now I should go. I've got plenty of other rivers to clean up, after all. Good-bye, Kirsty! Good-bye, Rachel! Thanks again."

The three friends hugged one another, and then Milly waved her wand. Kirsty and Rachel were whisked up in the sparkly whirlwind once more and went flying away at top speed.

Moments later, the two girls were back at Rainspell Lake. The first thing they noticed was that the tire had vanished from where they'd seen it earlier.

"Milly is a fast worker." Rachel laughed happily. "Isn't fairy magic amazing?"

"But we've got to do our part, too, just like she said," Kirsty reminded her. "Maybe we could write to some of the local factories and ask them to help keep rivers and lakes clean."

"That's a great idea," Rachel agreed. "And maybe we could . . . Oh! Look, Kirsty!"

Rachel was pointing to a clump of cattails near the water. Kirsty's eyes widened as she saw what was hidden inside. "It's our boats!" She squealed, leaning over and pulling them out. "Oh, and look, they're good as new again!"

Both girls examined their boats in delight. The paper was now smooth and dry, and the colors were fresh and bright. It was as if they were brand-new. And, thanks to Milly's magic, there were now a few fairy passengers drawn on the inside of the boats. The  tiny drawings were all smiling up at Kirsty and Rachel.

"I'm going to keep this forever," Rachel declared happily. "What a fun surprise!"

Rachel linked an arm through Kirsty's

and the two girls headed back toward their cottage. "Tomorrow is our last day here," Kirsty said, suddenly remembering. "And we still need to find Carrie the Snow Cap Fairy's wand." "I really hope we can," Rachel said. "The world already looks so much

better for having the Earth Fairies."

Just then, carried on the breeze, the girls both heard a tiny, faint tinkling sound. It sounded like Fairyland bells ringing. The girls looked at each other and grinned. "Sounds like the fairies agree with you, too," Kirsty said. "We really have to help Carrie find her wand tomorrow!"

Rachel and Kirsty found Nicole, Isabella, Edie, Coral, Lily, and Milly's missing magic wands. Now it's time for them to help

# Carrie
## the Snow Cap Fairy!

Join their next adventure in this special sneak peek. . . .

# Frosty Leaves

*"Brrr!"* Shivering, Rachel Walker glanced across the bedroom at her best friend. Kirsty Tate was just waking up, too. "It's really cold this morning, isn't it?"

Kirsty yawned and nodded. "It's freezing," she agreed. "It's been getting colder all week."

"Well, I suppose it *is* getting late in the

year," said Rachel. She sat up in bed, wrapping the comforter around her shoulders. "It'll be winter soon—but I didn't expect the weather to change quite so fast!"

"Haven't we had a wonderful vacation though, Rachel?" Kirsty sighed happily. "It's been so special to come back to Rainspell Island, where we first met."

The Walkers and the Tates were spending the fall break together in a pretty little cottage on beautiful, magical Rainspell Island.

"Yes, it's been fabulous!" Rachel smiled. "And we're even having another fairy adventure, just like the first time we visited Rainspell."

"Only this time it was *our* turn to ask the fairies for help," Kirsty pointed out.

When Kirsty and Rachel had returned

to Rainspell Island a week ago, they'd been horrified to see the wide, golden beach covered in litter. So they'd asked the king and queen of Fairyland if their fairy friends could help them clean up the human environment.

The king and queen had explained to the girls that fairy magic could only do so much, and that humans had to help the environment, too. But they had agreed that the seven fairies who were about to complete their training could become the Earth Fairies for a trial period. They would work together with Rachel and Kirsty to try to make the world a cleaner place. If the fairies completed their training successfully, protecting the environment would become their permanent task.

But just as the Earth Fairies were about

to be presented with their new wands,
Jack Frost and his goblins had zoomed
toward them on an ice bolt. The goblins
had snatched all seven wands, and then
Jack Frost's icy magic had sent them
tumbling into the human world.

# RAINBOW magic™

# Which Magical Fairies Have You Met?

- ❑ The Rainbow Fairies
- ❑ The Weather Fairies
- ❑ The Jewel Fairies
- ❑ The Pet Fairies
- ❑ The Dance Fairies
- ❑ The Music Fairies
- ❑ The Sports Fairies
- ❑ The Party Fairies
- ❑ The Ocean Fairies
- ❑ The Night Fairies
- ❑ The Magical Animal Fairies
- ❑ The Princess Fairies
- ❑ The Superstar Fairies
- ❑ The Fashion Fairies
- ❑ The Sugar & Spice Fairies

## ■SCHOLASTIC

Find all of your favorite fairy friends at
**scholastic.com/rainbowmagic**

HiT entertainment

# RAINBOW magic™
## SPECIAL EDITION

# Which Magical Fairies Have You Met?

**3 stories in each one!**

- ☐ Joy the Summer Vacation Fairy
- ☐ Holly the Christmas Fairy
- ☐ Kylie the Carnival Fairy
- ☐ Stella the Star Fairy
- ☐ Shannon the Ocean Fairy
- ☐ Trixie the Halloween Fairy
- ☐ Gabriella the Snow Kingdom Fairy
- ☐ Juliet the Valentine Fairy
- ☐ Mia the Bridesmaid Fairy
- ☐ Flora the Dress-Up Fairy
- ☐ Paige the Christmas Play Fairy
- ☐ Emma the Easter Fairy
- ☐ Cara the Camp Fairy
- ☐ Destiny the Rock Star Fairy
- ☐ Belle the Birthday Fairy
- ☐ Olympia the Games Fairy
- ☐ Selena the Sleepover Fairy
- ☐ Cheryl the Christmas Tree Fairy
- ☐ Florence the Friendship Fairy
- ☐ Lindsay the Luck Fairy
- ☐ Brianna the Tooth Fairy
- ☐ Autumn the Falling Leaves Fairy
- ☐ Keira the Movie Star Fairy
- ☐ Addison the April Fool's Day Fairy

## ■ SCHOLASTIC

Find all of your favorite fairy friends at
**scholastic.com/rainbowmagic**

HIT entertainment

RMSPECIAL12